Snow Bunny's Christmas Gift

Rebecca Harry

nosy crow

Snow Bunny
lived in the forest, with her friends
Mouse, Fox and Bear.

One snowy morning
just before Christmas,
Snow Bunny knotted the ties
on her little red cape and set
off to find her friends.

Mouse, Fox and Bear were
all ready for a day full of fun.
"What shall we do?"
asked Mouse.

"I know," said Snow Bunny.
"Let's go sledging on Honey
Hill. It's the perfect place!"

And off they went.

Soon Snow Bunny,
Mouse, Fox and Bear
were racing down Honey Hill.

Wheee! It was such fun . . . but the
winter wind blew and blew.

"I'm ch-ch-ch-chilly," said Mouse after a while.
"I want to go home." And off she scampered.

Snow Bunny, Fox and Bear felt sad.
"What shall we do now?" asked Fox.

"I know," said Snow Bunny.
"Let's go skating on Shining Lake.
It's the perfect place!"

And off they went.

Snow Bunny, Fox and Bear looped
and twirled across the ice.

Whizzzz!

But grey clouds soon covered the winter sun.

"I'm c-c-c-cold," Fox whimpered after a while.
"I want to go home." And off he trotted.

Snow Bunny and Bear
felt very sad.
"What shall we do now?"
asked Bear.

"I know," said Snow Bunny.
"Let's gather pine cones in
Treetop Forest.
It's the perfect place!"
But just as they reached
the forest, huge snowflakes
began to fall.

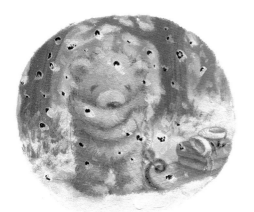

"I'm f-f-f-frozen," Bear
shivered after a while.
"I want to go home."
And off he trudged.

Snow Bunny felt sadder
than ever. "What shall I
do now?" she sighed.
"All my friends have gone.
I'll just have to go home
all by myself."

Night was falling and
Snow Bunny was nearly home
when, suddenly, she stopped.
Something was glinting
in the snow.

It was a bright, silver coin,
sparkling in the moonlight.
"Ooooh!" said Snow Bunny,
and she popped the coin in the pocket
of her cape. "What shall I do now?"

And, all of a sudden, she had a wonderful idea.
"I know the perfect place!" she said.

And off she went.

Snow Bunny reached Mr Badger's
shop just as it was about to close.
"Oh, please, Mr Badger," said Snow Bunny,
holding up her silver coin, "I just need one thing."

"What would you like?"
said Mr Badger.

"Please may I have one of
those?" Snow Bunny asked,
pointing to a shelf.

Then clutching her parcel,
Snow Bunny hurried home
through the dark.

Back in her cosy cottage,
Snow Bunny set to work.
All night long, as the icy
wind blew, and the grey
clouds covered the winter
sun, and the snow fell,
she knitted and knitted
and knitted . . . until she
had used up **all** of the
big ball of red wool
she had bought.

Finally, everything
was ready.

The next day was Christmas
Day, and Snow Bunny set off
through the glittering snow.
First she went to Mouse's
house. "I've brought you
a gift," she said.

Mouse unwrapped her parcel.
Snow Bunny had knitted her a
little hat with a pompom
on top. "Thank you,"
Mouse smiled.
"Now I won't be chilly!"

Then Snow Bunny went to Fox's house.
"I've brought you a gift," she said.

Fox unwrapped his parcel. Snow Bunny had knitted him a long,
woolly scarf. "Thank you," Fox grinned. "Now I won't be cold!"

Finally, Snow Bunny arrived at Bear's house.
"I've brought you a gift," she said.

Bear unwrapped his parcel.
Snow Bunny had knitted him
a cosy waistcoat with
a big, shiny button.

"Thank you!" Bear laughed.
"Now I won't be freezing!" And he gave
Snow Bunny a big bear hug.

Later, when the sun was setting, Snow Bunny
and her friends set off to light the candles
on the Christmas tree.

Snow Bunny wore her cape. Mouse wore her
little hat with the pompom on top. Fox wore
his long, woolly scarf. And Bear wore
his cosy waistcoat with the
big, shiny button.

They all had a lovely time.
"But we don't have a gift for you, Snow Bunny,"
said her friends.

Snow Bunny looked at her friends, so warm and snug in their new clothes, and smiled. "I don't mind one bit," said Snow Bunny . . .

" . . . because friendship is the greatest gift of all. Merry Christmas, everyone!"

For Jon, with love xxx

R.H.

First published in 2014 by Nosy Crow Ltd

This edition published in 2014

The Crow's Nest, 10a Lant Street

London SE1 1QR

www.nosycrow.com

ISBN 978 0 85763 350 7 (HB)

ISBN 978 0 85763 359 0 (PB)

Nosy Crow and associated logos are trademark

and/or registered trademarks of Nosy Crow Ltd.

Text copyright © Nosy Crow 2014

Illustrations copyright © Rebecca Harry 2014

The right of Rebecca Harry to be identified as the illustrator of this work has been asserted.

A CIP catalogue record for this book is available from the British Library.

Printed in China

Papers used by Nosy Crow are made from wood grown in sustainable forests.

1 3 5 7 9 8 6 4 2 (HB)

1 3 5 7 9 8 6 4 2 (PB)